BIG, FAT, The Bald Head!

MW00905361

Nancy Horton
Illustrated by Carter Horton

THE BIG, FAT, BALD HEAD!

Copyright © 2011 Nancy Horton

All rights reserved. Neither this publication nor any part of this publication may be reproduced or transmitted in any form or by any means, electronic or mechanical, including photocopying, recording or any information storage and retrieval system, without permission in writing from the author.

Scripture quotation marked NIV was taken from the Holy Bible, New International Version®, NIV® Copyright © 1973, 1978, 1984, 2010 by Biblica, Inc.™ Used by permission. All rights reserved worldwide.

ISBN: 978-1-77069-252-7

Word Alive Press
131 Cordite Road, Winnipeg, MB R3W 1S1
www.wordalivepress.ca

Library and Archives Canada Cataloguing in Publication

Horton, Nancy Jane
      The big, fat, bald head! / Nancy Horton, Carter Horton.

ISBN 978-1-77069-252-7

      1. Cancer--Patients--Family relationships--Juvenile
literature. 2. Cancer--Chemotherapy--Juvenile literature.
I. Horton, Carter, 1997- II. Title.

RC264.H67 2011   j362.196'994   C2011-900623-5

Although written for children whose loved one is undergoing chemotherapy, to help them cope, prepare for its effects, and help increase faith and hope, this book is a good educational book for any child.

This book is dedicated to my husband Robert and our three sons, Ben, Carter, and Spencer, who learned to look past my appearance and into my heart!

My mom is the best mommy that could ever be. She makes me smile and laugh and helps me feel good about being me!

1

My mom has beautiful,

long,

blond

hair

that I like to braid and twirl.

I like to fix her **hair** up, **play,**

and pretend she's a little girl.

4

One day she went to the doctor, came
home and told me she was ill.

Right away she needed surgery and had
to take several kinds of pills.

I cried, because the medicine my mom had to take would make all her pretty hair fall out, make her tummy feel sick, and sometimes make her too weak to play.

I felt mad and sad and thought it was unfair!

Every three weeks, she went to the hospital, where they injected chemotherapy into her veins by IV, while Grandma watched and played with me.

After this procedure my mom stayed in bed to rest her weary head. Sometimes we snuggled, read books, and watched TV until her strength returned.

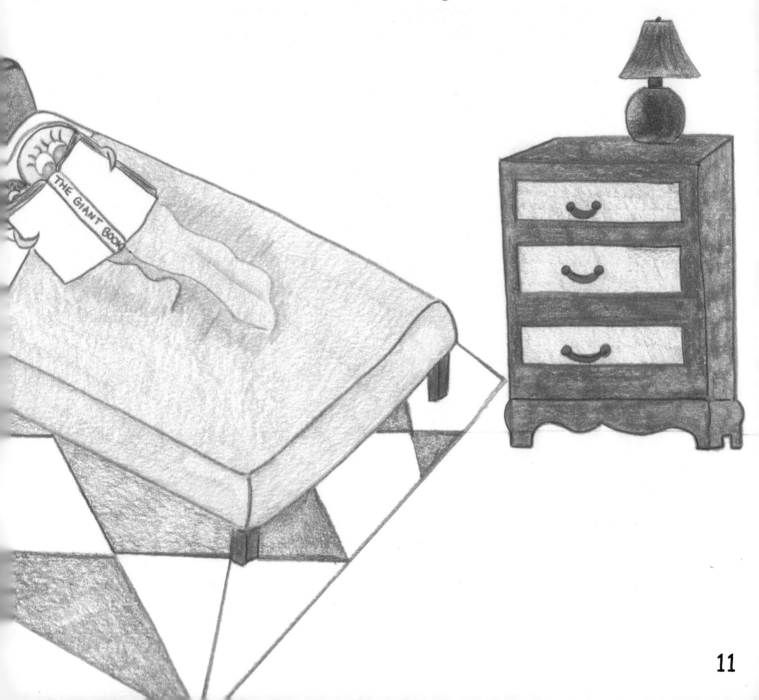

The white, porcelain bowl in the bathroom

became her new best friend,

until her tummy settled and she

stopped barfing again!

Her hair fell out after two short weeks of the first chemo dose, but I told her not to worry, she's still my mom and I love her just the same. Even with her "BIG, FAT, BALD HEAD!" I'd rub and kiss it with no shame!

My mom has had eight treatments now, and
the doctor says the cancer is all gone.

One year later...

Surprise!

My mom has new hair now!

It's brown, curly and long.

I can braid it up and play

again because she is now healthy and strong!

"O LORD my God, I called to you for help and you healed me." (Psalm 30:2, NIV)

Dictionary

Chemo (Chemotherapy): a mixture of medicine given to destroy cancer cells.

Doctors: God-given helpers on earth that help people get better!

Injected: medicine put into the body through a needle or syringe.

IV (Intravenous): a means of putting medicine into the body, through a person's veins.

Medicine: pills or liquid that help repair the body or take pain away.

Porcelain bowl: a toilet! (Used to go to the bathroom or throw up in.)

Procedure: a series of steps taken to accomplish a goal.

Surgery: an operation to remove tumours or cancer cells.

Veins: tubes in the body that carry blood around.

LaVergne, TN USA
28 February 2011
218212LV00004B

9 781770 692527